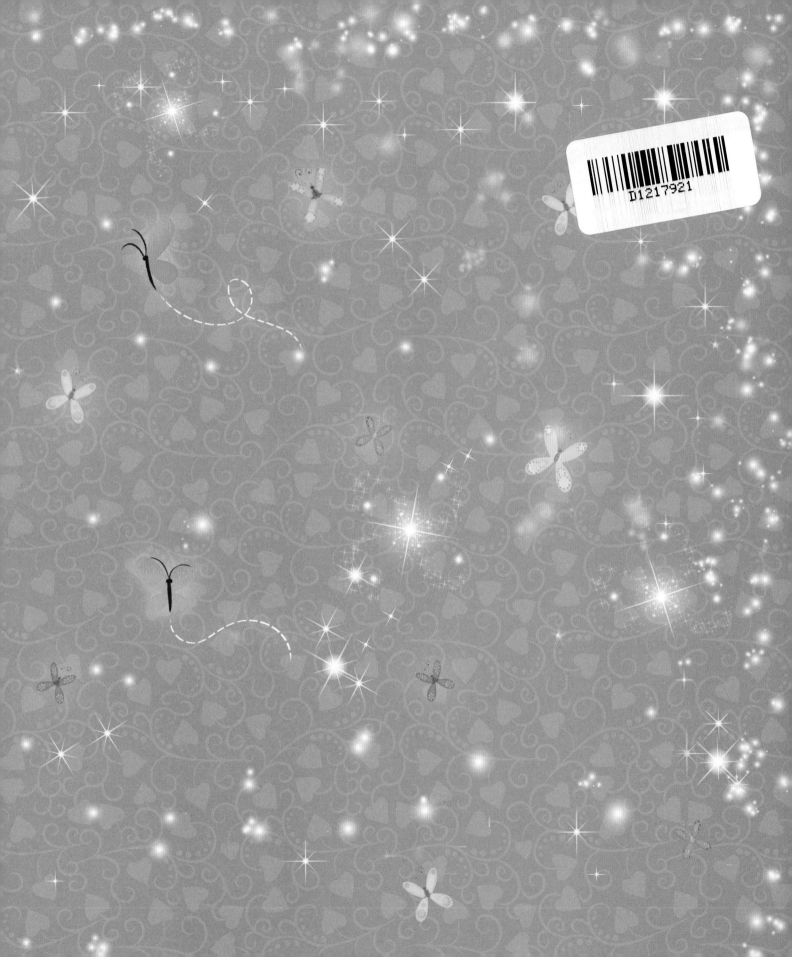

This igloo book belongs to:

....

igloobooks

Published in 2016
by Igloo Books Ltd
Cottage Farm
Sywell
NN6 0BJ
www.igloobooks.com

Copyright © 2016 Igloo Books Ltd

HUN001 0716
2 4 6 8 10 9 7 5 3 1
ISBN: 9781785576430

Illustrated by:
William Alvarez
Jacqui Davis
Sara Foresti
Ria Kim
Bonnie Pang

Written by Gemma Barder

Cover designed by Alex Alexandrou
Interiors designed by Stephanie Drake
Edited by Melanie Joyce

Printed and manufactured in China

My Beautiful Treasury of Fairy Stories

igloobooks

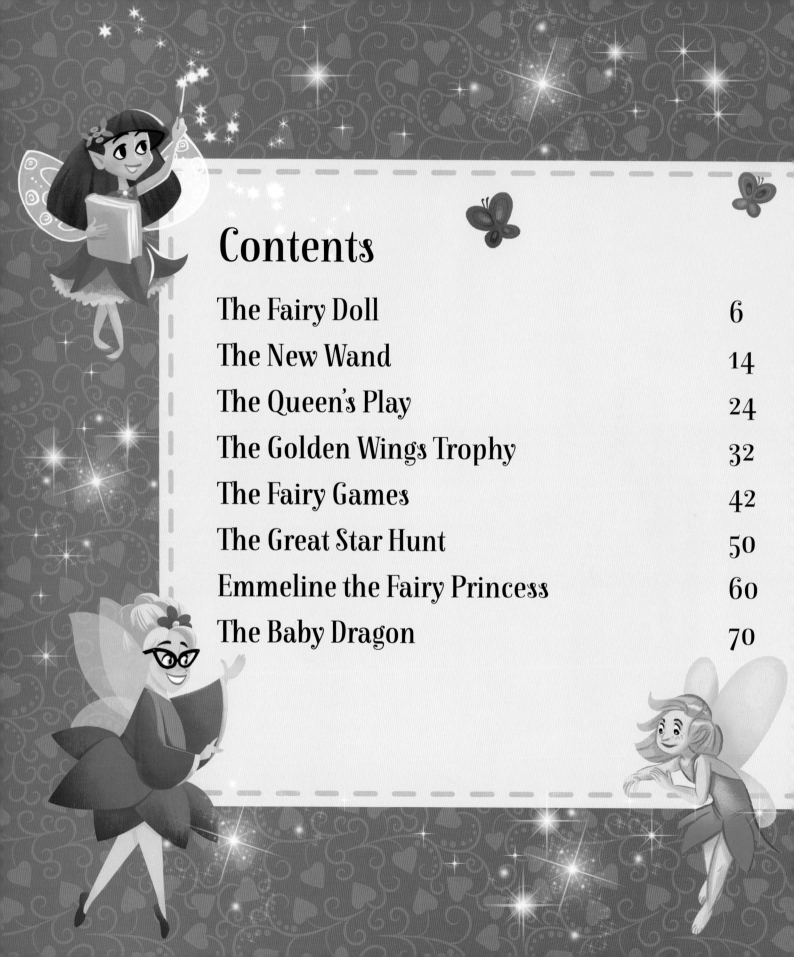

Contents

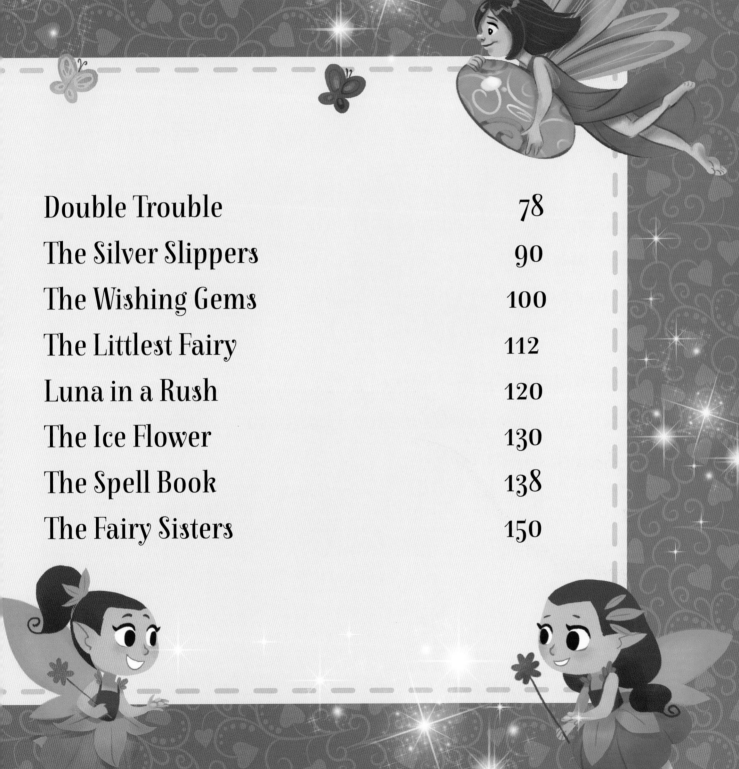

The Fairy Doll

Alice and Lucy were two little fairy sisters. They liked the same things and went everywhere together. Lucy and Alice never argued and were the very best of friends.

Then, one day, they decided to walk to the fairy market to spend their pocket money. It was there that they spotted the most beautiful fairy doll either of them had ever seen. "She's wonderful," sighed Alice. "I wish we could take her home."

But the fairy doll was very expensive. "I know," said Lucy, fluttering up and down. She'd had an idea. "If we use both our pocket money, we could buy her together!"

Alice agreed it was a marvellous idea. The two sisters bought the doll and flew home as fast as they could.

 At first, the sisters played together happily with their new doll. They had a lovely tea party in the garden, but after a while each wanted to play something different. "I think we should plait Dolly's hair now!" Lucy said, rushing off to find a brush and some ribbons. Alice didn't think that was a good idea at all. In fact, she had another idea entirely.

"Where's Dolly?" asked Lucy, as she returned with her comb and her pretty satin ribbons.

"She's sitting on her throne, of course," replied Alice. "I've decided we should play princesses now."

Lucy was furious. She wanted to plait Dolly's hair! Lucy waited until Alice was busy sorting out Dolly's clothes. Then, she quietly took out her wand and with a whoosh, she magicked Dolly into the air!

The Fairy Doll

When Alice realized Dolly was missing she flew into Lucy's bedroom in a temper. "Have you taken Dolly?" she demanded.

Lucy quickly hid Dolly behind her back. "Um... no..." said Lucy, telling a fib.

Alice knew Lucy wasn't telling the truth. So, she whipped out her wand and fizzed a spell behind Lucy's back, throwing the lovely doll high into the air.

"I want Dolly to play with me!" cried Alice, hugging Dolly tightly.
"But I want Dolly to play with ME!" cried Lucy even louder.

Suddenly, both fairy sisters were pointing their fairy wands at
Dolly, desperately trying to pull her towards them. Their magic
crackled in the air, as Dolly hovered above the fairies' heads.
Then all of a sudden... Rrrrrrip!

Their beautiful fairy doll had been torn in two. Alice and Lucy dropped their wands and ran towards where she lay. "Look what we've done," sniffed Lucy, wiping away a tear. "We should never have argued. Whatever shall we do?"

"We'd better tell Mummy," said Alice. She picked up the dolly pieces and headed downstairs to where their mother was busy in the garden, making fairy dust.

The Fairy Doll

Alice and Lucy's mummy shook her head when she saw the broken doll. "The only way to fix the doll is to work together and mend your friendship, too," she said.

So, the sisters pulled out their wands again. This time they both held hands, mixed their magic and wished as hard as they could. With a sparkle the doll mended!

From that day on, Alice and Lucy never argued again. They played with the doll together and decided that sharing was always best.

The New Wand

One morning, Fairy Daisybell was very excited. Soon, she would be going to Wand School. "I can't wait!" she cried, twirling around on her tiptoes excitedly. Suddenly, Daisybell noticed a prettily wrapped package on the kitchen table. "Grandma left it for you," said Mum. "It's for Wand School."

Daisybell fluttered her wings and tore open the parcel. Inside was a beautiful, jewel-encrusted wand. "A new wand!" she squealed.

"It's actually a very old wand," explained Daisybell's mother. "Your Grandma has owned this wand since she was a little fairy and it is very special. It can do wonderful magic, but you must be careful how you use it. If you wait for Grandma to come, she'll show you exactly what you need to do."

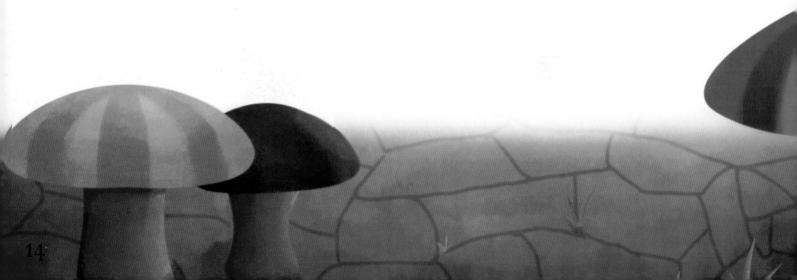

But Daisybell was impatient. She didn't want to wait. She grabbed the wand and headed straight for the garden to try out the magic. One of Daisybell's special charms was to turn the vegetables from her mother's vegetable patch into delicious, juicy berries.

Daisybell raised the wand and quickly muttered the charm. Zwoosh! A glittering stream of multi-coloured sparkles shot from the end of the wand.

The New Wand

Instead of a pile of delicious strawberries and blueberries, Daisybell changed the vegetables into icky, sticky, slimy snails! "Oh no!" cried Daisybell, frowning at the wand. "Why isn't it working properly?" Daisybell raised the wand again and tried a disappearing charm on the snails, but that didn't work, either.

Instead of making the snails disappear, Daisybell had turned them into great big, warty toads! "Ugh!" wailed Daisy as the toads hopped about. "This silly wand can't do anything right," she said, her face turning scarlet with anger. Daisybell rolled up her sleeves. She was going to MAKE the wand do what she wanted. She took a deep breath and shouted the disappearing spell one more time as loud as she possibly could.

⊙ The New Wand ⊙

The wand fizzed and crackled and sparks began to shoot from the very tip. She felt the grass rumble beneath her slippers as giant thorns started to sprout up all over the lovely garden lawn. "Oh, this is hopeless!" Daisybell fumed, throwing the wand down in a fit of temper. She was so upset, she didn't see a figure at the garden gate.

"What on earth has happened here?" said a kind voice. It was Daisybell's grandma.

"Grandma!" Daisybell cried, fluttering into her Grandma's arms. "It's all gone wrong. This silly old wand won't do what I tell it to do," she sniffed. "It must be broken."

Daisybell's grandma hugged Daisybell and picked the wand up from the floor. "It isn't broken, my love," she said kindly. "Let me explain."

The New Wand

Daisybell and Grandma found a spot between the hopping toads and prickly thorns. "It's a very special wand," began Grandma. "It produces great magic, but only if the fairy who uses it is calm, quiet and thoughtful. Charms that are cast in a rush or in anger will do the exact opposite of what the fairy wants them to do."

❧ The New Wand ❧

Daisybell's grandma took a deep breath and smiled. She waved the wand gently across the sky leaving a sparkling rainbow trail behind her. Tiny stars rained down on the lawn and slowly the spiky thorns melted away, leaving a lush, green lawn in its place. "That's amazing!" said Daisybell, feeling much calmer. "Would it be okay if I tried again? I do so wish to learn how to use it properly."

☙ The New Wand ☙

With the help of her grandma, Daisybell tried the disappearing charm once more. She took a deep breath and slowly said the magic words. The same rainbow trail and tiny, sparkling stars shot out of the wand and landed on the toads. With a fizz and a 'POP!' they were gone and the vegetable patch was back to normal. "Thank you, Grandma," Daisy said with a hug. "This is the best wand I've ever had."

The Queen's Play

"Gather round, fairies!" called Miss Flutterbug. "I have some very exciting news." Fairy Sally and her friends all gathered round and sat at Miss Flutterbug's feet. "The Fairy Queen has asked us to put on a special play to celebrate her birthday and you've each got a part in the show." All the fairies squealed and fluttered up and down with delight. Everyone, that is, apart from Sally.

Sally loved performing. In fact, she loved it so much that she practised singing and dancing in front of the mirror in her bedroom every night. The only trouble was, that as soon as Sally stepped in front of an audience, she became so nervous that she turned into a clumsy bag of nerves. "Must everyone join in?" Sally asked, shyly. "Of course!" replied Miss Flutterbug. "It's the queen's special birthday wish."

The fairies started rehearsals in a whirl of excitement. The play was about a princess who gets lost in the woods. Sally had the part of a squirrel who helps the princess find her way home. Every time she came on stage, however, Sally was so nervous, she mixed up her words and tripped over the scenery. "I'm going to ruin the play for everybody," thought Sally, sadly.

The night of the play soon came around and Miss Flutterbug's class was waiting nervously backstage. The Fairy Queen arrived and took pride of place on the front row. The show was about to begin!

The first half seemed to go very well, or so Miss Flutterbug thought. Then, to her surprise, as she peeked out at the audience from backstage, she saw the Fairy Queen was yawning!

"Fairies, fairies!" Miss Flutterbug announced during the interval. "You must all try extra hard in the second act. Oh, and Sally..." Miss Flutterbug looked kindly at Sally. "... Do try not to fall over."

This made Sally more nervous than ever. When the time came for her to go on stage, she stumbled forward and tripped over the scenery, nearly knocking over the fairy playing the princess.

"Oh no!" whispered Miss Flutterbug, but as she glanced over to the Fairy Queen, she could see she was pointing and laughing. Sally saw it too and jumped to her feet to say her line. "The forest is brave, but I am scary. Follow me!" Sally had got her line all mixed up, but the Fairy Queen began to giggle. She loved Sally's silly performance, even if it wasn't going to plan.

Sally decided it was probably best if she got off the stage as quickly as possible, but her squirrel tail got caught in the scenery and sent two cardboard trees crashing to the floor. By this time the queen was holding her tummy with laughter. She laughed even harder when Sally got tangled up in the stage curtain and pulled it down, on top of the other fairies.

The Queen's Play

Sally rushed off stage. "I'm so sorry, Miss Flutterbug!" she said. Just then, the Fairy Queen appeared. "I haven't laughed so much in ages!" she said to Sally. "What a talented little fairy you are. Come and take a bow. You certainly deserve it."

Everyone clapped and cheered as Sally took a bow. The play was a success after all!

The Golden Wings Trophy

"Is she here yet?" asked Fairy Neve as she fluttered up and down with excitement. Neve was waiting for her wonderful Aunt, Fairy Pumpernickel, to arrive for a visit. Fairy Pumpernickel wasn't just any Aunt, she was the most famous, most magical fairy in the Enchanted Forest. She had won the special Golden Wings Trophy three times in a row for creating new and exciting spells.

Ding-dong! went the doorbell. Fairy Pumpernickel had arrived. Neve squealed and flew into her Aunt's arms and gave her a hug. "Please can I see it? " asked Neve, fluttering around excitedly. Fairy Pumpernickel smiled. "Very well," she replied and out of a special box, she took the Golden Wings Trophy.

The Golden Wings Trophy

The trophy was made from the brightest, glittering gold Neve had ever seen. It was so shiny you could see your face in it, and the wings were so delicate Neve was sure they could flutter away by themselves. "Wow!" said Neve, holding the trophy close. "Is it okay if I play with it for a while?"

"Only if you take VERY good care of it," warned Neve's mother.

"I will!" called Neve as she whisked the trophy up to her bedroom.

Fairy Neve played with the trophy for hours. She pretended she had won it herself and made a funny speech in front of the mirror. When it came time for supper, Neve looked at the trophy, sadly.

No one at school would believe that her aunty was the real Fairy Pumpernickel... unless... Neve quickly stashed the trophy in her satchel. Her aunt wouldn't miss it for one day, would she?

The next morning, Fairy Neve fluttered to school before breakfast. She couldn't wait to see her friends and show them the famous Golden Wings Trophy. As she opened her satchel a beam of light filled the classroom. "Wow!" cried Angel, one of Neve's best friends. "It's so pretty!" Neve loved all the attention the trophy was getting and promised to show more fairies at lunchtime.

❧ The Golden Wings Trophy ❧

News of the famous trophy had spread around the entire school. So much so that when lunchtime came, a crowd of excited fairies was waiting for Fairy Neve. Neve gasped when she saw everyone. "Show us the trophy!" they cried. "Um… okay," said Neve as she nervously held the trophy above her head.

Fairy Neve was worried. Perhaps bringing the trophy to school wasn't such a good idea after all. Before she had a chance to put the trophy safely back in her satchel, it was magicked from her hands by an older fairy. "I just want to hold it!" said the fairy, flying away, but she hadn't had it long before it was tugged out of her hands by someone else!

Soon, the trophy was being snatched and fought over. Neve tried desperately to grab the trophy, but it was no use. It was flying around from one fairy to another until … Craaack! One of the delicate wings splintered and fell off. "Oh no!" cried Neve as the squabbling fairies quickly fluttered away. "It's ruined! What am I going to say to Aunt Pumpernickel?"

~ The Golden Wings Trophy ~

At home, a very nervous Neve confessed about taking the trophy. "Now it's broken," she said. "I'm so sorry, Aunt Pumpernickel." Neve thought her aunt would be very angry, but she wasn't. Aunt Pumpernickel said Neve should always ask permission before taking anything, but that some magic would put things right. So, she waved her wand...

The Golden Wings Trophy

"That's amazing!" cheered Neve as the broken trophy began to mend. "I think you should take this back now." Neve handed the trophy to her aunt with a smile. "The next time I hold that trophy, I want it to be because I have won it for myself. After all, I will have learned from the best fairy in the forest, my Aunt Pumpernickel!"

The Fairy Games

"Let the Fairy Games commence!" shouted Miss Buttercup, the headmistress of Enchantment School. All the fairies fluttered their wings and looked forward to a day of fun, games and excitement. The last race would be the Fairy Dash and then the Grand Cup would be presented to whichever fairy had won the most races. Fairy Eloise and Fairy Martha were two little fairies who were absolutely determined to win.

THE FAIRY GAMES

The first game was an egg-and-wand race. The fairies lined up
at the start, each balancing an egg on the flat of their wands.
The fairy who finished first without dropping their egg,
and without using magic, was the winner.
Eloise looked at Martha. "May the best fairy win,"
she said, smiling.
"I plan to!" said Eloise, smiling back.

The whistle blew and Eloise and Martha took off. They were neck and neck at the front until Eloise gave Martha's arm a nudge and Martha's egg tumbled onto the grass. "She did that on purpose!" thought Martha, as she put the egg back on her wand. Up ahead, Martha smiled as she crossed the finish line and won the race.

⊙ The Fairy Games ⊙

Next up was the Petal Pocket race. Each fairy jumped inside a tulip bud and paddled down the stream. Martha made sure she was next to Eloise as the whistle blew to start the race. Now it was Martha's turn to get her own back. As the fairies reached a bend in the stream, Martha gently tipped Eloise's tulip just enough to send Eloise splashing into the water.

The Fairy Games

Each fairy was determined to outdo the other. Eloise added heavy stones to Martha's beanbag in the beanbag toss, so Martha raised Eloise's bar in the flutter-jump competition. Eloise put soap on Martha's climbing shoes and she slipped off the obstacle course, so Martha hid Eloise's swimming costume just before the start of the swimming race. The two fairies battled all day until it was time for the final competition of the day. The Fairy Dash!

❧ The Fairy Games ❧

"Good luck, fairies!" said Miss Buttercup. "To the very top of the great oak tree and back again. On your marks, get set… go!" Eloise and Martha shot off as fast as their wings could carry them. Martha was determined Eloise wouldn't beat her. "I might have been a bit naughty today," thought Martha, "but Eloise started it!" Eloise was in the lead when Martha had an idea.

"Look out, Eloise!" Martha cried. "A big, hairy spider!" There wasn't a spider at all, but Eloise was so shocked she flew sideways, hit her wing on a branch and landed with a thump, in a bird's nest. Now Martha was in the lead! However, as Martha glanced backwards, she could see Eloise was hurt. "Oh no!" she thought. "I must go back and make sure Eloise is okay."

"I'm so sorry!" Martha said, fluttering back to the nest.

"I'm sorry, too," said Eloise, sadly. "I just wanted to win."

"We've both been silly," said Martha, "but let's finish the race!"

The rest of the fairies were zooming past them, but Eloise and Martha didn't care. They held hands and took off together, finishing the race in joint last place. It didn't matter though, because now they would be best friends forever!

The Great Star Hunt

It was the day of the Great Star Hunt and the fairies in the forest were fluttering with excitement. "Come on, Lily!" called Fairy Phoebe to her little sister. "I don't want to be late!"

In the Great Star Hunt, the fairies searched the forest for an enchanted, gold star, hidden by the Fairy Queen. Whoever found the star first was granted a special wish as her prize.

Lily was very excited, as it was her first time taking part. "I'm just a bit nervous," she whispered, as they fluttered to the starting line by the old oak tree. "What would you wish for if you won, Phoebe?"

Phoebe smiled and replied. "To keep the magic star! What would you wish for?" Before Lily could reply, the sisters saw that the Fairy Queen had arrived.

The Great Star Hunt

"Is everybody ready?" said the queen, smiling at all the fairies.
"Then I declare this year's Great Star Hunt... begun!" The Fairy
Queen's wand began to glow and a trumpet sounded. All the little
fairies started fluttering their wings and dashing off in different
directions around the forest.

⊙ The Great Star Hunt ⊙

Phoebe was a very fast flyer and was soon up at the treetops, while little Lily was still on the forest floor. In the whirl of wings and excitement, Lily had felt a little dizzy, and now she was left staring as every other fairy had flown off to search. Lily picked herself up, brushed down her wings and dashed off after Phoebe.

As the hunt got into full swing, little Fairy Lily wasn't having much luck at all. She had caught her wings on a thorny bush, fluttered straight through a cobweb and been knocked and nudged by the older fairies in the hunt.

"Oh, this is just hopeless!" cried Lily. "I'm never going to find the star. " Soon, Lily spotted a big, pink toadstool and sat down underneath.

She hugged her knees, sadly and watched as the older fairies carried on looking for the star.

Meanwhile, Phoebe was having a great time! She loved dashing around the forest and was sure she was going to win.

Phoebe was just thinking about where she could look next when her friend Ellie flew by. "Hello, Phoebe!" she called. "This is so much fun! Is Lily enjoying it?" Ellie looked around. "Where is Lily? I haven't seen her since the start."

Phoebe stopped suddenly. Where was Lily?

Fairy Phoebe was so busy having fun, she hadn't noticed her little sister was nowhere to be seen. Phoebe really wanted to win the Great Star Hunt, but she felt worried about Lily. She might even have been knocked over. So Phoebe swooped down to the forest floor and decided to search for Lily, instead of the star.

The Great Star Hunt

Phoebe heard someone crying under a toadstool. It was Lily.
"I'm sorry, I've spoiled the star hunt. I couldn't keep up," she sobbed.

Phoebe hugged her sister. "The star hunt doesn't matter," she said.
"You are more important." Phoebe pulled Lily to her feet. As she
did, Phoebe noticed something golden sticking out from behind
the stalk of the toadstool.

"It's the star!" squealed Phoebe with delight. "You found it!" Lily jumped up and down with excitement. "No, you found it!"

Phoebe threw her arm around her little sister. "WE found it!" she said, giving Lily a squeeze. The two fairies flew as fast as they could, back to the oak tree, clutching the shimmering star and smiling at one another. When they arrived at the oak tree, Lily took the star and proudly handed it to the Fairy Queen.

⊙ The Great Star Hunt ⊙

"What would you like for your wish?" asked the Fairy Queen. Lily smiled and said, "For Phoebe to keep the star!"
"Your wish is granted," said the queen, waving her wand.

Lily handed the star to a delighted Phoebe. "Thank you for being my big sister and coming to find me," she said. "I can't wait for the Great Star Hunt next year!"

Emmeline the Fairy Princess

Emmeline lived in a beautiful castle, high up in the fairy hills. She had everything a fairy princess could wish for, a room full of toys, a gigantic squishy bed and a jewel-encrusted wand. And yet, Emmeline was NOT happy. "Humph!" pouted Emmeline one day. "These toys are BORING! Why don't I have any exciting toys to play with? It's NOT FAIR."

Emmeline flung open her wardrobe. "Humph! The same old BORING dresses. I never get anything new. It's NOT FAIR!"

Downstairs, the breakfast gong rang. "Oh no," said Emmeline as she pulled out a dress and slammed the wardrobe door closed. "It's breakfast time. I bet it will be the same old huge banquet of buttery pastries, piles of chocolate-chip muffins, stacks of toast and gallons of fairy tea. BORING!"

"Good morning, Emmeline!" said the Fairy Queen happily, as Emmeline stomped into the room. "We've got such an exciting day ahead of us. First we're going to open a new wand shop, then we're going to be fitted for new tiaras and then we're off for a ride in the royal carriage so we can say hello to all our subjects! Doesn't that sound like lots of fun?"

Emmeline didn't think that sounded like much fun at all. "Humph!" she said, squashing a half-eaten muffin in her hand. "Why do I have to do all these BORING things? I wish I could do something easy like... bake muffins and cakes all day, like the palace cook. She's got it SO easy."

That night, the Fairy Queen decided to make her daughter's wish come true.

After a day of tiresome waving and boring ribbon-cutting, Emmeline climbed into her big bed (but not before she had moaned about her pillows being too soft).

She fell into a deep sleep, so deep in fact that she didn't notice the Fairy Queen placing a special spell on her. "Emmeline wants to cook and bake, let's see how she feels when she's awake!" she whispered with a smile.

When Emmeline awoke the next day, she was no longer in her comfortable bedroom, she was in the palace kitchen! "How did I get here?" she wondered.

Emmeline didn't have time for wondering. The butler was walking towards her looking very flustered. "Cook! Stop dawdling, you've got muffins to bake, bread to slice and crumpets to toast!" Emmeline realized the butler was talking to HER and he had no idea who she really was!

Emmeline got stuck in, kneading the bread and baking the muffins.

At first it was lots of fun, MUCH more fun than riding around in a boring old carriage. But soon, Emmeline's arms began to ache.

She singed her wings on the crumpet toaster and by the time breakfast was ready, Emmeline was ready to go back to bed.

"Where do you think you're going?" asked the butler, carrying a pile of dirty dishes on a tray. "It's time to make some pies for lunch and after that, you need to wash all these dishes."

Emmeline had never washed up in her life, and as for making pies? She didn't know where to start. Her pastry was lumpy, the filling was too sloppy and when she finally got them into the oven, they burned to a cinder.

By the end of the day, Emmeline was exhausted. She realized just how lucky she had been when all she had to do all day was wear beautiful dresses and perform her Fairy Princess duties. Oh, how she wished she could go back to that life! As she wished, her eyes began to droop and she nodded off with her arms deep in the soapy water.

Early next morning Emmeline jumped up. "I've got to get the bread in the oven!" she cried, then realized she was back in her own big, squishy bed. Just then, the Fairy Queen knocked on the bedroom door and Emmeline fluttered into her arms. "I'll never moan about being a princess ever again!" said Emmeline. And from that day on, she never did.

The Baby Dragon

In the magical forest, Fairy Tilly and her friends were fluttering home from Enchantment School, chatting about their day. They were passing by the stream when suddenly, Tilly noticed something glimmering. "Whatever could it be?" Tilly gasped as she fluttered to the water's edge. All the little fairies followed her and soon they had gathered around the mysterious object.

The object was green and blue, with swirling patterns on it. Tilly thought it was the most beautiful thing she had ever seen. "It's an egg!" said Fern, a very clever little fairy. "I'm sure I've seen a picture of it in one of my books. We'd better leave it here."

All the fairies agreed, except Tilly, who was worried that no one would come for the beautiful egg.

⌒ The Baby Dragon ⌒

That evening, Tilly fluttered back to the water's edge to fetch the egg. It was still there! She fluttered home, cradling the egg in her arms, as fast as her wings could carry her. She made a cosy corner for it in her bedroom and tucked it in with a warm blanket. Tilly kept watching the egg until her eyes felt droopy and she fell fast asleep.

The next morning, Tilly awoke to a very strange sound. 'CRACK...'
The egg was beginning to hatch! Tilly fluttered over to the corner of
her room just in time to watch the cutest little baby dragon she had
ever seen appear from inside the shell. He rubbed his eyes and Tilly
gave him a big hug. "We're going to have so much fun!" she cried.

Tilly soon realized that it wasn't easy looking after a baby dragon.
He was very mischievous. When Tilly heard her mother coming
upstairs with a cup of fairy tea, she hid the baby dragon in her
wardrobe. When she opened it up again, the baby dragon had
scorched her dresses! And the trouble didn't end there...

⦿ The Baby Dragon ⦿

Tilly decided to take the baby dragon into her garden for some fresh air, but he trampled over the roses and his tail got twisted in ivy!

When Tilly tried to make him some supper, the baby dragon ended up eating everything in the kitchen!

Later on, when Tilly was trying to do her enchantment homework, the baby dragon swallowed the end of her wand with a great 'gulp!' and hiccupped magic sparkles for an hour!

The Baby Dragon

"Oh, dear," said Tilly, as the dragon breathed clouds of sparkly smoke and fire. She immediately ran to tell her mother exactly what was going on. Although she was shocked to discover a real baby dragon had been living in her fairy house, Tilly's mother knew just what to do. "We need to take the dragon back to the stream," she said gently. "His mother may be looking for him."

The Baby Dragon

At the water's edge, Tilly and her mother did not have to wait long before the sky went dark and a much bigger dragon swooped down and landed by the stream. The baby dragon scampered towards her happily. Tilly saw how happy the baby dragon was and knew in her heart that she had done the right thing. She hugged her mother tightly and it was the best feeling ever. The baby dragon thought so, too!

Double Trouble

It was a beautiful spring morning. "I'm going to have a day of fun!" cried Fairy Trixy, but then she glanced at the calendar. "Oh no!" she cried. Today was the Fairyland Spring Clean. That meant all the fairies had to help sweep leaves and clean away cobwebs. "Do I have to?" Trixy moaned. "The spring clean is so boring!" Trixy's mother smiled. "All the fairies will be there, it might be fun!"

Trixy couldn't believe that sweeping away a bunch of old, dry leaves could be anything other than dull. Then, she came up with an idea. "I wonder if there's a way I could go to the clean-up and have lots of fun, too." Then, Trixy noticed Mum's spell book was open on the kitchen table. "There must be something in here," she thought.

◌ Double Trouble ◌

When Mum wasn't looking, Trixy took the spell book upstairs. She soon came across just the spell she was looking for... a fairy double spell. "All I have to do is say a few magic words. Before I know it there will be two of me!" Trixy grabbed her wand and recited the spell... "Be her fun or be her trouble, make me a fabulous fairy double!"

PING! To Trixy's amazement, a smiling fairy who looked just like her appeared. "Yippee! It worked," cried Trixy. "Off you go to the Spring Clean," she said. "I've got far more fun things to be getting on with today!"

Trixy's double nodded and fluttered off to join her family, who were just about to leave. No one knew that the real Trixy was hiding and giggling as everyone left.

First, Trixy decided to make pancakes for breakfast. She laid out all
the ingredients and couldn't wait to eat a whole stack of pancakes
all to herself. Then she realized she had never made pancakes by
herself before. Trixy's mother had always done it for her. Trixy gave
it a go, but the pancakes didn't taste right and they got stuck to the
ceiling when she tried to flip them.

❧ Double Trouble ❧

Meanwhile, at the Spring Clean, Trixy's double wasn't behaving herself in quite the way she should. She had spotted a row of neatly piled leaves and was swooping from one pile to the next, sending leaves flying everywhere. The real Trixy didn't know it yet, but the spell had taken her naughtiness and put it into her trouble-making double!

~⊙ Double Trouble ⊙~

Back home, the real Trixy looked at the pile of messy, sad-looking pancakes she had made. "Oh well," she sighed. "I'll go and pick some blackberries instead," and she fluttered off with her basket.

The blackberry bush was full of juicy berries, but Trixy wished her friends were there to share them. So she decided to head to the fairy playground instead.

⊙ Double Trouble ⊙

Back at the Spring Clean, Trixy's double had got tired of jumping in leaves. Instead she had decided it was time for an early lunch. There were tables full of fairy food and berry juice laid out for the helpers, and best of all, lots of cream cakes. Trixy's double helped herself to plates full of food and cakes!

At the fairy playground, no one was playing on the swings and no one was slipping down the slide. All of Trixy's fairy friends were helping out at the Fairyland Spring Clean! Trixy sat on a tree stump. She'd thought getting out of the clean-up would be lots of fun, but now she wished that she could be with everyone instead of feeling alone and bored.

Trixy decided it was time to tell the truth. She fluttered into the forest to find her family, but was horrified to see her double greedily chomping on cream cake while the other fairies were hard at work. Suddenly, someone called out, "Those cakes are for our lunch, you naughty fairy!"

"Oh, dear," thought the real Trixy. Something had gone very wrong.

Trixy took her double by the hand and led her to where her mother was tidying a toadstool patch. Trixy's mother was a bit surprised, but Trixy soon explained what she had done. "Now I understand," said Trixy's mother. "This naughty little fairy has been causing mischief all morning!"

"I'm sorry," said Trixy. "I thought it would be fun if my double was here instead of me, but I missed everyone!"

◎ Double Trouble ◎

Trixy's mother took out her wand and reversed Trixy's spell. Trixy's double disappeared. "I think it's time the real Trixy got stuck in and helped," said Mum, handing Trixy a bag and a broom. "I know it's not much fun, but..."

"That's okay!" said Trixy with a grin. "I'm going to have so much fun working hard, you'll think there are two of me!"

The Silver Slippers

It was the end of another day at Fairy School, but Fairy Eva didn't feel happy at all. That morning, Fairy Willow had walked into the classroom wearing a wonderful pair of fairy slippers. They were as white as snow, with two cherry red pom-poms on the toes. Eva had gasped in amazement and everyone agreed they were the nicest ones they had ever seen.

As she flew home, Fairy Eva thought about her own tatty slippers. She wondered if she should have chosen new ones for her birthday instead of her new bracelet. Eva loved the bracelet, but she couldn't stop thinking about Willow's new shoes. Suddenly, she noticed something shiny peeking out from under a bush. It was a pair of beautiful, sparkly, silver slippers!

"Oh my goodness!" cried Fairy Eva, carefully picking the slippers up. They were so pretty and they looked like they would fit her.

Eva decided she would take the slippers to show her mother, then perhaps they could find out who they belonged to. Before going into her house, Eva couldn't resist trying the lovely slippers on. "I'm sure whoever they belong to wouldn't mind," she thought.

The Silver Slippers

The slippers felt so wonderful, that when Eva got home she didn't tell her mother about them right away. Instead, she fluttered up to her bedroom and admired them in the mirror.

The slippers went with all the dresses in Eva's wardrobe and they were the most comfortable things she had ever put on. Eva put the slippers under her bed for safe-keeping. "Maybe, whoever these slippers belonged to doesn't want them anymore?" she wondered.

⊙ The Silver Slippers ⊙

The next day, Eva was having breakfast. She had decided not to tell her mother about the slippers just yet. She wanted to invite all her fairy friends to come over so she could show them off. Then, as Eva lifted a spoonful of porridge to her mouth she realized her bracelet was missing! "My bracelet, it's gone!" she cried, Fairy Eva felt very upset because she loved her bracelet. So Eva and her mother began to search the cottage.

They searched and searched until finally, Eva's mother found the bracelet under Eva's bed. It had slipped off when Eva was hiding the slippers there. Eva felt happy, but also, a bit sad. "Whatever is the matter?" said Eva's mum, giving her a hug. "I thought you'd be so happy now we've found your bracelet!" Then, Mum noticed the shiny slippers. "Where did these come from?" she asked.

"Oh, Mummy," said Eva. "I found them in the forest. I was going to tell you so we could find their owner, but they were so pretty I wanted to keep them for a while. When I lost my bracelet, I realized just how awful the little fairy who lost the slippers would be feeling, too."

Eva's mummy gave her a hug. "I'm glad you told the truth,"
she said, "but we do need to return the slippers." She told Eva
to do a drawing of the slippers, which she magically transformed
into lots of leaflets. With a whoosh of her wand, Eva's mummy
sent the leaflets flying around the fairy village.

The Silver Slippers

It didn't take long before someone knocked at the door. Outside, a fairy was fluttering up and down excitedly. "Thank you!" cried the fairy, putting the slippers onto her feet. "They must have fallen out of my school bag. Where did you find them?" Eva told the fairy the whole story. She thought the fairy would be angry at her, but instead, she gave her a great big hug.

⊙ The Silver Slippers ⊙

From that day on, Fairy Eva took very good care of her bracelet.
She realized that looking after the lovely things she had was much
more important than feeling sad about the things she didn't have.
The following week was Eva's birthday and she asked for a charm
to go on her bracelet. When she opened the little gift box, she saw
the most beautiful charm of all, a pair of pretty, silver slippers!

The Wishing Gems

Fairy Primrose had really enjoyed her birthday. Mum had made a delicious cake and invited Primrose's friends to a super-fun party where she'd made up lots of fun games to play. Best of all, Primrose's mum had wrapped a pile of presents to open. It had been a perfect party and now Primrose's mother was exhausted. She sat down and put her feet up for a quick rest.

Primrose let out a long sigh. "Whatever is the matter?" asked Primrose's mother, yawning.

"I had such a lovely party," sighed Primrose. "I wish I could do it all over again."

"Why don't you play with some of your presents?" said Mum. Primrose had been given a new mirror, some sweets, a beautiful new dress and a toy wand. They were all lovely, but not as lovely as opening new presents!

Just then, the delivery-fairy knocked on the door. "Parcel for Miss Primrose!" she called.

The parcel was a birthday gift from Primrose's Great Aunt Violet who lived a long way away. Primrose fluttered with excitement as she ripped off the brown paper to reveal a small, wooden box. Inside the box were three glittering gems. "They're beautiful!" Primrose gasped. "What could they be?"

☙ The Wishing Gems ☙

In all her excitement, Primrose did not see the letter her Great Aunt Violet had put in the package. "They're wishing gems," said Primrose's mother, picking up the letter. "Each gem will give you one wish."

"Yippee!" cried Primrose. "I can wish for anything I like!"
"Be careful," said Primrose's mother. "Aunt Violet says the gems are very powerful..."

Primrose wasn't listening and she grabbed the little box and rushed out into the garden.

"Hmm," thought Primrose. "What shall I wish for first?" Then it came to her. "Of course!" Primrose picked up one of the gems, squeezed it tightly in her hand and said, "I wish I could have lots of cake and presents every day." Suddenly, Primrose's garden was filled with a twinking light. When Primrose opened her eyes again her garden was overflowing with cakes and presents!

Primrose spent the rest of the day opening the huge pile of gifts and eating the delicious cake. She went to bed feeling very happy, if a little bit sick from all the cake she had eaten. Primrose's mother was left to pick up all the discarded wrapping paper and put the uneaten cakes in the bin. It took her a long time, but eventually she finished and fell asleep in her chair.

The Wishing Gems

The next morning, Primrose awoke to find that her bedroom had been filled with even more cakes and more presents. She couldn't believe how lucky she was, it was like having a birthday every day! Primrose began to rip open the presents again, but she soon found that opening presents could get a bit tiring, and eating cake for breakfast, lunch and dinner was actually getting a bit boring.

The next day, more gifts and cakes appeared. Fairy Primrose didn't have enough time to open all the presents, so they bulged out of cupboards and drawers. She certainly couldn't eat all the cakes, and the icing was starting to make the whole house feel sticky. There was nothing for it. Primrose had to use another wish. She picked out a gem, squeezed it tightly and said, "I wish all these cakes and gifts would disappear!"

In a whoosh of sparkles, the cakes and presents disappeared into thin air. Primrose was left with only the gifts she had been given on her birthday. She sighed happily and opened the wooden box to look at the last gem. Primrose was just wondering what to do with her last wish when her mum appeared carrying a large bag.

"Thank goodness all that cake's gone!" she said. "Have you thought about what you are going to wish for next?"

"I just can't think," replied Primrose. "Will you help me?"

Primrose's mother gave her a quick hug. "I wish I could, but I've got to take all that leftover wrapping paper to the recycling centre."

Suddenly, Primrose knew what her last wish would be. When her mum returned home, she opened the door to find the cottage was sparkling clean. Everything was tidy and all the bowls and cups had been put away. "Goodness!" gasped Primrose's mother. "Did you use your last wish to clean the cottage?" she asked.

Primrose grinned. "No, I did the cleaning," she said. "I used my last wish for this." Behind Primrose was the comfiest armchair her mother had ever seen. There was even a foot rest so she could put her feet up. "Here's a cup of tea," said Primrose. "Now it's your turn to be spoiled. I couldn't think of a better way to say thank you, or to use my last wishing gem!"

The Littlest Fairy

Fairy Lilac's family had one thing in common. They were all very small indeed. They were so small they didn't need a tree hollow to live in, they just needed a toadstool. Lilac loved it that way. She could snuggle up in the cosiest corners and was unbeaten when playing hide-and-seek! In fact, Lilac thought being small was wonderful until her first day at Enchantment School.

Lilac fluttered nervously into the playground and looked around at the other fairies. They all towered above her and chattered happily to each other. Three fairies stood together and the one in the middle was a beautiful fairy called Peppermint. Lilac smiled shyly at her, but Peppermint didn't even realize she was there! Lilac sighed. Maybe being small wasn't so great after all.

The next day there was Flying Class. Lilac loved flying, so she took her place at the front of the class. Before Lilac knew it, Peppermint and her friends had whooshed past her, sending her into a spin.

The day after that was Cupcake Class. Lilac wanted to top her cakes with chocolate cherries, but the jar was out of her reach, and of course, Peppermint got there first.

The Littlest Fairy

By the end of her first week at Enchantment School, Lilac felt sad. When lunchtime came, she flew off by herself. "They probably won't even realize I've gone," she whispered, unhappily, as she fluttered off around the school grounds. When she returned, Lilac noticed a crowd of fairies gathered around the old wishing well.

"What in the stars is going on?" said Lilac, when she finally managed to tug at someone's wings and get them to notice her. "It's Peppermint!" said one of the older fairies. "She was showing off with her new wand when it fell down the well. Now it's stuck!" Lilac flew to the front of the chattering crowd. Peppermint was standing with Miss Flitter, looking very sorry for herself indeed.

The Littlest Fairy

"I'm sorry, Peppermint," said Miss Flitter. "The well is enchanted. My magic won't work. You'll have to climb down to get your wand."

"But... but..." Peppermint sniffed, "I wouldn't fit. I'd get as stuck as my wand if I tried to go down there!"

"Um, excuse me, Miss Flitter," said a little voice. Lilac had stepped out of the crowd. "Maybe I can help?"

Lilac fluttered to the edge of the well and stared down into it.
It looked very scary and smelled of old pondweed. She took a deep
breath and, in the loudest voice she could muster said, "I'm quite
small and I'm sure I could fly down and fetch the wand."

Everyone looked at Lilac. "Are you sure, Lilac?" asked Miss Flitter.
Lilac nodded bravely and fluttered down to the bottom of the well.

The well was dark and creepy, but Lilac was determined. With one scoop, she fished Peppermint's wand out of the smelly water and flew back up. "Well done, Lilac!" cheered Miss Flitter.
"Thank you, thank you!" cried Peppermint. "Without you, my wand would have been lost forever."

Lilac beamed. She had saved the day and all because she was the littlest fairy in school. Being small wasn't so bad after all!

Luna in a Rush

The Fairy Festival took place every year. It was the most exciting place to be because there were rides and stalls selling treats. Fairy Luna couldn't wait to meet her friends there. "Please can I go, please, please?" Luna begged her mother.

"Yes," replied Luna's mother with a smile. "However, I need you to do some errands for me first."

Luna sighed as she took the list from her mother. She had to post some letters, buy some berries and then take some biscuits to her grandma's cottage. "I'll go as fast as I can," thought Luna. "Then I won't miss any of the festival!"

⌒ Luna in a Rush ⌒

Luna crammed her basket with the letters, the biscuits and the gold coins. She flew to the postbox as fast as she could and reached inside the basket. But instead of finding the bundle of letters, Luna grabbed the shortbread biscuits and stuffed them through the letterbox! Luna was in such a rush that she even didn't notice the crumbs spilling onto the ground.

Luna in a Rush

Next it was time to buy some berries at the market. "Two bags of blueberries, please," Luna asked, hurriedly. "And could you be quick? I'm in a rush!" The market fairy handed over the bags, but instead of paying with the purse of coins as she was meant to, Luna handed over her mother's letters. Luna grabbed the berries and shot off to her grandmother's house, as the market fairy called after her.

At last, Luna reached her grandmother's cottage. "Hello Grandma!" Luna said breathlessly. "I can't stop to chat, I've got to get to the Fairy Festival, it's going to be so much fun, but don't worry, I've got your..." Fairy Luna reached into her basket, but the biscuits were nowhere to be seen. Luna's grandma peeked into the basket. "Berries? I thought you were bringing some yummy biscuits?" Grandma said.

Suddenly, Luna realized what she'd done. "Oh no!" she cried.
"Now I remember. I put your biscuits into the letterbox, which
means I must have given the letters to the market fairy and
that's why all I've got left is the berries."
"Why ever did you do that?" asked Luna's grandmother.
"I was doing everything too quickly," replied Luna.

"What am I going to do?" asked Luna, sadly.

"First you need to slow down," replied Grandma. "It's rushing around that got you into this mess."

Luna nodded. "What about the letters and the market? I don't think Mum will be very pleased when she finds out."

"Don't worry," said Grandma, fetching her shawl and giving Luna a big hug. "I'll help you sort everything out, as long as you promise not to go too fast!"

126

Luna and her grandmother fluttered back to the berry stall. Luna took a deep breath and slowly explained everything to the market fairy. Luckily, the market fairy was very kind and saw the funny side of Luna's story. She gave her the letters and took the gold coins instead. "I hope you make it to the festival!" she called.

Next, Luna showed Grandma the postbox surrounded by crumbs. "I'm afraid your biscuits are in there," Luna said, sadly, peering through the narrow letterbox. It all looked a little hopeless until Grandma calmly took out her wand and waved it this way and that. One by one, each of the biscuits floated out of the letterbox and back into Luna's basket.

"All that's left to do now is get you to the festival," said Grandma. Luna giggled happily. "Let's go to the festival together, it's not far from here," she said.

Luna's grandma smiled. "Won't I slow you down?" she asked.
"Not at all," replied Luna, linking arms with her. "I've learned that going slowly can sometimes be the best thing!"

The Ice Flower

Fairy Josephine was very excited. Her mum was taking a day off from her busy job as a flower-collecting fairy and they were going to make cupcakes together. "Chocolate or cranberry?" asked Josephine's mother, smiling.

Before Josephine could answer, someone banged on the door. It was a messenger from the palace. "The Fairy Princess has a terrible fever!" he cried. "The doctor says she needs a magical Ice Flower, right away!"

Josephine's mother grabbed her cloak. "I must fly to the Blue Mountain. It's the only place the Ice Flower grows!" she cried. "Please can I come, too?" pleaded Josephine, but Josephine's mother warned her that the Blue Mountains were too dangerous.

As Josephine watched her mother flutter away, she had an idea. "I'll show Mum how brave I am!" she thought, excitedly, and decided that she would go up the mountain, too.

Fairy Josephine fluttered along the winding path that led to a forest at the foot of the Blue Mountain. The forest was dark and echoed with strange noises. Tree branches cast scary shadows across the path and Josephine felt a bit nervous as she started to search for the Ice Flower. She could see daisies and tulips and some pretty snowdrops, but nothing that looked at all like the magical flower.

‿⟲ The Ice Flower ⟳‿

At last, Josephine reached the edge of the forest and began to climb the steep path that led up the mountain. There was lavender among the rocks and pretty heather, too, but the Ice Flower was still nowhere to be seen. "Perhaps I should climb higher?" thought Josephine, feeling a bit nervous. "Magical flowers might only bloom at the very top of the mountain!"

As Josephine climbed higher, a fierce wind blew and thick snow
began to fall. She wrapped her cloak around her, but it was
no use. Her wings had become so cold, she couldn't fly so Josephine
sat behind a rock, shivering and wondering what to do. She had
wanted to help find the flower and now she was lost and afraid.

Josephine looked down the mountain. She could see the fairy village in the distance. She wished she could be back in her nice warm cottage with a cup of hot chocolate. "I want my mum," she thought as she blinked back tears. Just then, she was sure she could see a sparkling blue light in the distance... someone flying towards her!

It was Josephine's mother! "Mum, I'm here!" Josephine cried. Josephine's mother swooped down and scooped up the little fairy. Together they flew to the bottom of the mountain where Josephine started to feel much warmer.

"Whatever were you doing up there?" asked Josephine's mother. Josephine explained how much she had wanted to help. "It's nice to help people," said Josephine's mother, "but helping others isn't any good if it puts you in danger."

Jospehine's mother hugged her. "Perhaps there is something you could help me with," she began. "I found some Ice Flowers at the top of the mountain. Let's take them to the palace together."

At the palace, the Fairy Queen was waiting for them. "Thank you!" she cried. "Now the princess will get better. I am so grateful. Won't you come in for tea?"
"Thank you, Your Majesty," replied Josephine's mother, "but we've got cupcakes to make!"

The Spell Book

Fairy Teal loved Spell Class. It was the lesson she loved most in the whole school day. Teal's spells teacher, Miss Cauldron, had given the class some very special homework and Teal couldn't wait to tell her mum. "Everyone has been asked to bring in their family's spell book!" Teal said excitedly.

"How exciting," said Teal's mother, taking their spell book from the cupboard. "This book has been in our family for years."
"It's all stained and tatty," said Teal. "I can't take that to school. Abigail's book cover has gold on it and Ginny's has a sapphire!"

Teal pleaded with her mother to buy a new spell book from the Enchanted Bookstore, but Teal's mother frowned. "You can't choose a new spell book in a hurry," she warned. "Let's go to the bookstore and see if they can tidy it up a bit."

The Enchanted Bookstore was almost closing when Teal and her mother arrived. Teal's mother took the family spell book to the book mender while Teal browsed the shelves full of magical books. Soon, Teal spotted a lovely spell book with a heart on the front. She looked at the price tag and it was exactly the amount of pocket money she had!

"I'd better be quick," said Teal, as she rushed up to the counter to pay for the book. Just as Teal was popping the book into her bag, Mum came up to her. "The book mender is going to see what he can do," she said, as they left the bookshop. "I'm sure he'll get it looking lovely." Teal felt a bit guilty, but she couldn't wait to show her new book off.

✥ The Spell Book ✥

The next morning, Teal sneaked her new spell book into her satchel and headed to school. She settled into her seat and gently placed the book on her desk, but as she opened the little lock, blue shooting stars shot out from the pages. They flew around the classroom sending Teal's classmates diving for cover. Teal finally managed to close the book just as Miss Cauldron arrived.

"Quiet now, fairies," Miss Cauldron called. "It's time to show your
spell books." One by one, each fairy went to the front of the class.
Holly Berrybush was just telling everyone that her spell book came
all the way from Peru, when there came a high-pitched singing
from Teal's desk. "Teal, please be quiet when Holly is talking," said
Miss Cauldron.

"It's not me, Miss," pleaded Teal. "It's my spell book!"

"Please make it stop," said Miss Cauldron kindly. Teal smiled weakly, but as she opened the book again, it sprang from her desk and started flapping around the classroom. "Come back!" cried Teal. "Oh, please come back," but the naughty book landed on the top of a tall shelf, flipped to the middle pages and started firing chocolate cupcakes at the fairies.

The Spell Book

Miss Cauldron and the rest of the class ducked under their desks to avoid the flying cakes. Teal waved her wand at the spell book and it stopped moving, but not for long. Soon it was up and flying around the room again. This time it was snapping its cover at a very startled Miss Cauldron. "Oh no!" cried Teal. "Why won't you behave? You're driving me batty."

No sooner had Teal spoken than the spell book flipped open and

bats flew all around the classroom! They got tangled in the fairies' hair and swooped in and out of the bookshelves. Teal waved her wand, but it didn't make any difference. "Teal!" cried Miss Cauldron, using her wand to deflect a bat that was headed her way. "What on earth is the matter with your spell book?"

Just then, Teal's mother opened the classroom door. "I'm sorry to disturb you, but... goodness! What on earth is going on?" Quick as a flash, Teal's mother opened the beautiful book she was carrying. She muttered a quick spell and the naughty spell book finally fell to the floor.

"Thank you!" cried Teal, as she ran to her mother. "That must be a pretty powerful book."

147

"It's our family spell book," said Mum. Teal couldn't believe it. The book mender had made their old, stained book look brand new, with a lovely soft, green cover. "I'm sorry, Miss Cauldron," Teal said in a sad voice. "This is my family spell book. I was ashamed to bring it in because it was all old and tattered, so I bought a new one from the Enchanted Bookshop."

The Spell Book

Miss Cauldron smiled. "New spell books need careful handling," she said. "When you are a bit older, I am sure you will pick the right one for you."

Mum gave the family book to Teal. "I'll take the other one back to the shop," she said. "Spell books are a bit like people. It's what's on the inside that matters."

"Thanks Mum," said Teal and she gave her a great big hug.

The Fairy Sisters

Fairy Elin loved to copy her sisters, Fawn and Pax. They were taller, had closets full of pretty clothes and always got to go to parties.

One afternoon, Elin's sisters were going to a wonderful dance in the forest clearing. Elin had pleaded with her mum to go, but Mum said that Elin was too little and that she could go to parties when she was older.

"It's not fair," thought Elin, as she watched her sisters getting ready. Then, she saw that they had left their wand boxes opens. That gave Elin an idea. Fawn and Pax's wands were much more powerful than Elin's... which was perfect for what she had in mind!

Elin sneaked the wands back to her room. Maybe if she got ready
too, her sisters would take her to the party. "First I'll need a dress!"
said Elin. She pointed Fawn's wand over her head and it erupted
with shooting stars. The stars whooshed in a circle around Elin,
but when she opened her eyes, Elin saw that her clothes had
been transformed into a gigantic, ugly ballgown!

The Fairy Sisters

The ballgown had so many bows and underskirts, that Elin could hardly move. "Fawn and Pax won't let me go to the party dressed like this!" Elin cried. She waved Fawn's wand one more time, but this time the magic was so strong it knocked her off her feet. As Elin slowly stood up, she saw that the ballgown was just as hideous as ever, but now it was torn all over.

The Fairy Sisters

"It must be this wand," said Elin, throwing Fawn's wand aside. Next, Elin picked up Pax's wand. "Time for a makeover!" she grinned, heading over to her sisters' dressing table. It was a bit tricky to sit down in the ballgown, but Elin managed to arrange her skirts under the table. "Give me a beautiful hairdo!" said Elin, tapping Pax's wand on top of her head.

Elin could feel the magic whirling in and out of her long hair. She couldn't wait to see what Pax's magic had done. Then, Elin saw her reflection. Her hair was now standing on end and had turned the brightest shade of blue she had ever seen. "My hair!" Elin cried, desperately trying to pat it back down on top of her head.

Just then, Elin heard her sisters chattering along the corridor. She quickly scooped up the wands and fluttered downstairs before they could see her. "Perhaps these wands aren't as powerful as I imagined," thought Elin. "Maybe if I used both wands together it would transform me into the most sophisticated, fashionable fairy ever!" With that, Elin held the two wands above her head and wished with all her might.

The Fairy Sisters

The wands began to shake in Elin's hands. Sparks fizzed and stars flew from the end of each wand. Soon a cloud of magic dust formed, covering Elin from head to foot. She shut her eyes as tightly as she could and waited for the magic to stop. When the wands finally stopped moving, Elin opened her eyes. She was sure the magic would have worked this time and she couldn't wait to see how she looked.

"Oh no!" Elin wailed as she looked at her reflection in the mirror. Her hair was still standing on end, but now it was like a rainbow! Her ballgown had doubled in size and she could barely see out of the mass of bright purple ruffles around her collar. Elin finally gave up. She was exhausted and the last thing she wanted to do now was go to a party.

Pax and Fawn were just about to the leave the cottage when they
spotted Elin. "Goodness! Who are you?" Pax asked the strange little
fairy with rainbow hair, in a huge ballgown. Elin was too ashamed
to answer. "That's a very interesting outfit," said Fawn.
"No it's not!" Elin sniffed, tears rolling down her cheeks. "It's awful!"
"Elin! Is that you?" Pax and Fawn cried together.

⊙ The Fairy Sisters ⊙

Elin told her sisters everything. Together, Fawn and Pax undid Elin's magic until she was back to normal. Then they helped their tired little sister up to bed. "There will be plenty of parties to go to when you are older," said Pax, kindly, but Elin shook her head. "I don't know about that," she yawned. "It all seems a bit too much like hard work!" With that, Fairy Elin fell fast asleep.